CUB REPORTER
MEETS FAMOUS AMERICANS

WHAT'S YOUR STORY, SACAGAWEA?

Ellen Labrecque
illustrations by Doug Jones

Lerner Publications ◆ Minneapolis

Note to readers, parents, and educators:
This book includes an interview of a famous American. While the words this person speaks are not her actual words, all the information in the book is true and has been carefully researched.

Lerner Publications Company
A division of Lerner Publishing Group, Inc.
241 First Avenue North
Minneapolis, MN 55401 USA

For reading levels and more information, look up this title at www.lernerbooks.com.

Main body text set in Avenir LT Pro 45 Book 15/21. Typeface provided by Linotype AG.

Content Consultant: Amy Mossett, Sacagawea scholar, Mandan/Hidatsa of North Dakota

Library of Congress Cataloging-in-Publication Data

Labrecque, Ellen.
    What's your story, Sacagawea? / by Ellen Labrecque.
        pages cm. — (Cub reporter meets famous Americans)
    Audience: Grades K–3.
    ISBN 978-1-4677-7966-1 (lb : alk. paper) — ISBN 978-1-4677-8535-8 (pb : alk. paper) — ISBN 978-1-4677-8536-5 (eb pdf)
    1. Sacagawea—Juvenile literature. 2. Shoshoni women—Biography—Juvenile literature. 3. Shoshoni Indians—Biography—Juvenile literature. 4. Lewis and Clark Expedition (1804–1806)—Juvenile literature. I. Title.
    F592.7.S123L33 2015
    978.0049745740092—dc23 [B]   2014044159

Manufactured in the United States of America
1 – VP – 7/15/15

Table of Contents

Sacagawea 4

Are you an explorer too? 6

What was your childhood like? 8

How did your life change after that? 10

How did you meet Lewis and Clark? 12

Where exactly did the corps plan to go? 14

Why did they pick you and your husband? 16

What was the journey like for you? 18

How did you help the Corps of Discovery? 20

What was the most important part of
    the trip for you? 22

When did you finally make it to the
    West Coast? 24

What happened on your return trip? 26

Why is your journey still important? 28

Timeline 29

Glossary 30

Further Information 31

Index 32

Hello, friends! I'm here to talk to a very famous American. Her name is Sacagawea. Let's hear her story! Sacagawea, why are you famous? Can you tell us about yourself?

Sacagawea says: Certainly. More than two hundred years ago, I helped two explorers, Meriwether Lewis and William Clark, travel across the American Northwest. Along the way, I helped our team survive. I found food to eat, made clothes, and sometimes kept the team from getting lost. I also helped Lewis and Clark talk to the people who already lived in the area.

Sacagawea helped explore the American Northwest in the 1800s. This painting shows what she may have looked like in the spring of 1805 while on her journey.

Are you an explorer too?

Sacagawea says: Not exactly. My people had already lived on this land for many years. I belong to the Shoshone (*sho-SHO-nee*) American Indian nation. I was born around 1788 in what is now the state of Idaho. The Shoshone were **nomads** at that time. This means we traveled from place to place. I knew the land very well.

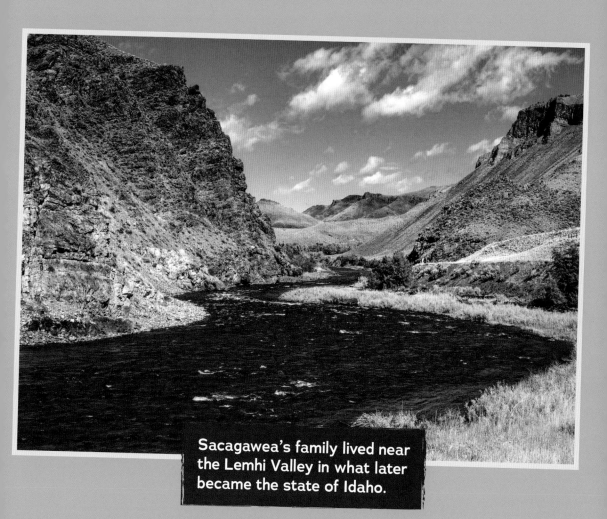

Sacagawea's family lived near the Lemhi Valley in what later became the state of Idaho.

What was your childhood like?

Sacagawea says: I grew up with my brothers and sister. We ate fish we caught. I was an expert at gathering wild plants to eat. We also ate wild animals that our people hunted, such as rabbits, elk, and buffalo. When we camped, we lived in a **tipi**. But when I was twelve years old, I was captured by members of the Hidatsa, an enemy nation. They took me 600 miles (1,000 kilometers) away from my homeland to their village in what is now North Dakota.

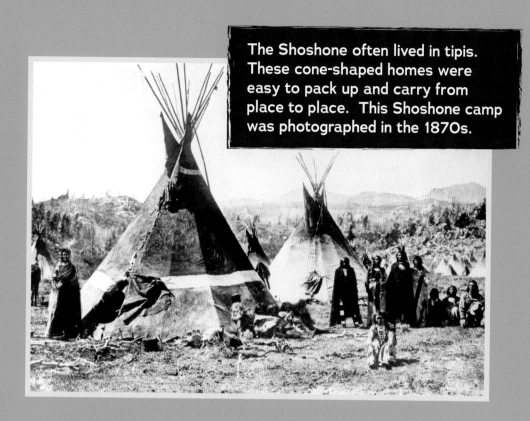

The Shoshone often lived in tipis. These cone-shaped homes were easy to pack up and carry from place to place. This Shoshone camp was photographed in the 1870s.

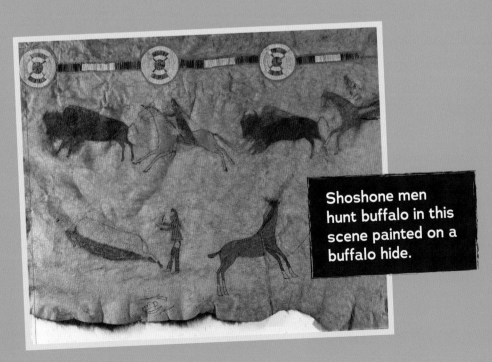

Shoshone men hunt buffalo in this scene painted on a buffalo hide.

How did your life change after that?

Sacagawea says: American Indians in this area often adopted their captives. The Hidatsa village became my home. I helped cook and make clothes. I took care of the babies and younger children. I also learned to speak the Hidatsa language. The Hidatsa gave me the name Sacagawea (*sah-KAH-gah-wee-ah*). It means "Bird Woman." A few years after I was captured, I married a French Canadian fur **trader**, who lived in the village. His name was Toussaint Charbonneau.

Artist George Catlin made this 1832 painting of a Hidatsa village in North Dakota. Sacagawea lived in this village after being captured and adopted by the Hidatsa.

How did you meet Lewis and Clark?

Sacagawea says: The United States had just bought a huge region of land west of the Mississippi River. But white Americans didn't know much about most of this land. So Lewis and Clark formed a group of explorers called the **Corps** of Discovery. This group began traveling through the newly bought land. The corps arrived at our village in late 1804. They needed help to explore the land.

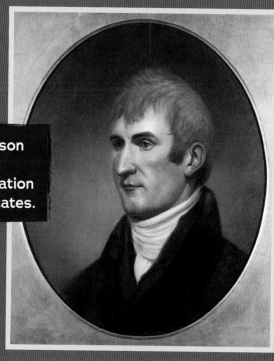

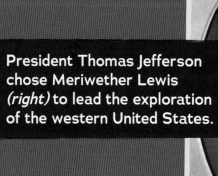

President Thomas Jefferson chose Meriwether Lewis *(right)* to lead the exploration of the western United States.

Meriwether picked his friend William Clark *(left)* to colead the Corps of Discovery. Their journey lasted from 1804 to 1807.

Where exactly did the corps plan to go?

Sacagawea says: They planned to travel west along the Missouri River, cross the Rocky Mountains, and reach the West Coast. White Americans had never been that far west before. Lewis and Clark didn't know what they would find along the way. They asked my husband and me to help them.

Lewis and Clark crossed rivers and mountains on their journey west. Thomas Mickell Burnham created this painting of their trip in the early 1850s.

Why did they pick you and your husband?

Sacagawea says: Lewis and Clark knew they would need horses to cross the mountains. My people, the Shoshone, had horses. Lewis and Clark hoped I could convince the Shoshone to trade their horses for other items. The corps members didn't speak Shoshone. But I spoke Shoshone and Hidatsa. My husband spoke Hidatsa and French. One corps member, Francois Labiche, spoke French and English. So we came up with a plan. I would **translate** the Shoshone language into Hidatsa. Charbonneau would translate Hidatsa into French. Labiche would translate French into English. That way, Lewis and Clark would know what the Shoshone people were saying.

This 1963 painting shows the Corps of Discovery making plans with Sacagawea and her husband at the Hidatsa village.

What was the journey like for you?

Sacagawea says: We left our Hidatsa village in the spring of 1805. I was the only woman in the group. I had just had a baby, Jean Baptiste, two months earlier. I had to care for him during the journey. We traveled in boats on the river. I usually sat in a **canoe** with my baby. Sometimes I walked along the riverbank and carried him on my back. We traveled up to 20 miles (32 km) a day!

Sacagawea brought her son, Jean Baptiste, on the journey west. Here she starts a fire to cook a meal.

How did you help the Corps of Discovery?

Sacagawea says: We often met other American Indian groups. These people didn't know if they could trust the corps. But when they saw that I—an American Indian woman—was with the corps, they were less worried. I helped convince them that Lewis and Clark would not harm them. I also found berries, roots, and plants that were safe to eat. And I stayed calm when things went wrong. Once a gust of wind almost knocked our canoe upside down. Medicine, **maps**, and other supplies fell into the water and started to float away. I calmly reached into the water and saved many items. Captain Lewis said that if I hadn't done this, the trip could've been ruined!

The Corps of Discovery traveled by boat for much of their journey. They often met groups of American Indians. In this 1905 painting, Charles Marion Russell imagines Sacagawea *(standing, right)* speaking to other American Indians.

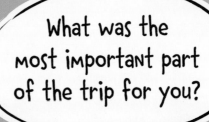

What was the most important part of the trip for you?

Sacagawea says: That summer, we arrived in the area where I grew up. Soon we met the Shoshone. My older brother, Cameahwait (*Ka-ME-ah-wait*), was now my people's leader. I was so happy to see him again! And I convinced him to give us horses in exchange for battle-axes, knives, and clothing. Without those horses, we couldn't have carried all our supplies over the giant mountains ahead of us.

Sacagawea introduces her son, Jean Baptiste, to her brother Cameahwait.

When did you finally make it to the West Coast?

Sacagawea says: We got there in the fall of 1805. I saw the ocean for the first time! I even saw a whale. We built a fort and spent the winter living on the coast. We made clothes and shoes called **moccasins** for our return trip. We used the salt from the ocean to add flavor to our elk meat and to help keep it fresh. In the spring of 1806, we finally turned back east.

Sacagawea and the corps spent the winter at Fort Clatsop in Oregon. This modern replica of the fort was built based on plans that Captain Clark drew in his journal.

A Shoshone person made these moccasins out of buffalo hide with hair and buckskin ties in the 1870s.

What happened on your return trip?

Sacagawea says: We took a different route on our way back. But I knew this part of the Rocky Mountains. My people had been here often. So once again, I helped guide the corps. Captain Clark called me his pilot. A few months later, we reached the Hidatsa village where Charbonneau and I lived. My husband, son, and I stayed there. The rest of the corps kept going the way they had come.

This mural was painted by Edgar Paxson in 1912. Paxson imagines Sacagawea pointing out a route to Lewis *(center)* and Clark *(left)*.

Why is your journey still important?

Sacagawea says: The Corps of Discovery explored lands that no white Americans had ever seen. But the corps might not have survived without me. Many white men would not have expected an American Indian woman to know so much or to make such a difference on our journey. Today the United States honors me in many ways. I have more landmarks and memorials built in my honor than any other woman in American history. Many mountains and lakes are named after me too. I helped Lewis and Clark learn much about these western lands.

Timeline

1788 Sacagawea is born around this time.

1800 Sacagawea is captured by Hidatsa Indians around this time.

1803 or 1804 Sacagawea marries Toussaint Charbonneau.

February 11, 1805 Sacagawea's first child, Jean Baptiste, is born.

April 7, 1805 Sacagawea joins Lewis and Clark's Corps of Discovery.

May 14, 1805 Sacagawea saves important supplies and papers from the Missouri River.

August 16, 1805 Sacagawea briefly reunites with her Shoshone family.

November 7, 1805 The Corps of Discovery reaches the Pacific Ocean.

August 17, 1806 The Corps of Discovery arrives back at Sacagawea's Hidatsa village.

December 20, 1812 Sacagawea dies from illness.

Glossary

canoe: a long, narrow boat that is moved by someone using a paddle

corps: a large group of people working together

maps: drawings that show where places are

moccasins: soft leather shoes

nomads: people who move from place to place

tipi: a cone-shaped home made from animal skin

trader: someone who gives away items in return for items of equal value

translate: to listen to words spoken in one language and repeat them in a different language

Further Information

Books

Jazynka, Kitson. *National Geographic Readers: Sacagawea.* Washington, DC: National Geographic Children's Books, 2015. Find out more about Sacagawea's life.

Napoli, Donna Jo. *The Crossing.* New York, Atheneum, 2011. Explore Sacagawea's story through the eyes of Jean Baptiste Charbonneau, Sacagawea's baby.

Nelson, Maria. *The Life of Sacagawea.* New York: Gareth Stevens, 2012. Learn more about Sacagawea in this illustrated biography.

Websites

Lewis and Clark for Kids
http://mrnussbaum.com/lcflash
This website about the Corps of Discovery has videos, maps, timelines, fun facts, and more.

Montana Kids—Sacagawea
http://montanakids.com/history_and_prehistory/lewis_and_clark/sacagawea.htm
Learn about Sacagawea's life before and after she became a guide for Lewis and Clark.

National Geographic—Go West across America
http://www.nationalgeographic.com/west
Travel west across America with Sacagawea, Lewis, and Clark.

Index

Charbonneau, Jean
  Baptiste, 18, 23
Charbonneau, Toussaint,
  10, 16, 26
Clark, William, 4, 12, 14,
  16, 20, 26, 28
Corps of Discovery, 12, 16,
  20, 26, 28

Hidatsa, 8, 10, 16, 18, 26

Labiche, Francois, 16
Lewis, Meriwether, 4, 12,
  14, 16, 20, 28

Shoshone, 6, 16, 22

Photo Acknowledgments

The images in this book are used with the permission of: © Michael Haynes- www.mhaynesart.com, pp. 5, 19, 23; © Witold Skrypczak/Lonely Planet Images/Getty Images, p. 7; © Werner Forman/CORBIS, p. 9 (bottom); © Ben Wittick/Buyenlarge/Getty Images, p. 9 (top); © INTERFOTO/George Catlin/Alamy, p. 11; Independence National Historical Park, p. 13, all; © Buffalo Bill Center of the West/Art Resource, NY, pp. 15, 25; State Historical Society of North Dakota Museum Collection 1985.22, p. 17; © Peter Newark American Pictures/Bridgeman Images, p. 21; © Connie Ricca/CORBIS, p. 25 (top); © Buffalo Bill Center of the West/Art Resource, NY, p. 25 (bottom); The Granger Collection, New York, p. 27.

Front cover: © Michael Haynes- www.mhaynesart.com.